SCARLET

LEAF

REVIEW

ESSAY &

SHORT-

STORY

AWARDS

SCARLET LEAF

PUBLISHING

HOUSE

2016

ISBN: 978-1-988397-02-3

PUBLISHED BY SCARLET LEAF PUBLISHING HOUSE

Toronto, Canada

Contents

ESSAY AWARDS

FIRST AWARD

CREATION, OR VIRTUAL MULTIPLE PERSONALITY DISORDER

BY *KATE VAN DER MEER*

*Author's biography: **Kate** is an emerging writer who loves her personal anonymity.*

I play videogames. A lot. Maybe not lots of different ones, but I do play them a lot. More than I should: they are my favorite form of procrastination. Until about a year ago, I kept my distance from MMOs – massively multiplayer online games. I knew from friends, from YouTube, and from common sense after having been browsing the Internet for years that the MMO atmosphere could at times be quite tense. By that, I mean you could run into a chat channel with either intense or offensive subject matter, or your party (of which most MMOs make it almost a requirement to be a part in order to advance through some quests) could get more or less worked up about your messing up, slow reaction times, misclicks, or anything else that might happen. Worked up – read: explosive.

I'm not a great player. If we're into honesty and all that, I'm barely a good player. Attention span – that's an issue. Planning ahead – sometimes an issue. Reaction time – definitely an issue. Seeing everything around me – don't even get me started on how huge of an issue that is. Prioritizing the best skills (or even remembering them at some point) – definitely an issue. Misclicks due to either one of pets, sudden spasms, annoying wires, lag, lack of attention, so on and so forth – that happens to everybody…. Right? Anyway, you're getting the point by now. I mess up. A lot.

And I also like to avoid being told that even more. Especially when it comes from rage-filled gamers whether in all-caps in the party chat or screaming through whatever voice chat client is being used. Especially when it comes from people I don't know – who sometimes become a part of your party whether you want it or not. Have you started wondering by now how is any of this related to the title? I'm getting to that now. Soon. Until about a year ago, I mostly stuck to single-player games – spacing out is one of the main reasons why I play games sometimes and they definitely allow for it, if you're playing the right game, such as a turn-based strategy game. My favorite, since childhood, has been the Heroes of Might and Magic franchise, of which there are now many games and they have both the option of single and multi-player. It's probably also the one game I'm actually good at. Actually good at – read: better than my friends whom I've dragged into liking it, but still suck at compared to the masters out there. And no, I'm pretty sure I'm not selling myself short here.

I've also, of course, experimented with Co-op games. For the most part, those I've played make it easy to play just with your friends – big groups aren't a requirement and some games have NPCs – non-playable characters, in one word, bots – whose roles you don't need to fill in order to play. They're not the sharpest tools in the shed, but they get the job done relatively decently.

About a year ago, I watched an anime. Sword Art Online. Long story short: virtual MMO where a headgear allows you to be in the game world much like in a dream, but everyone is stuck there with the only way to get out being to defeat the final boss – no easy feat, by the way (it actually takes them two years and, compared to me, they are gods at this). Unreasonably, that made me want to try MMOs. Best idea ever, right?

Here we get to how all this relates to the title. Around the same time, a friend asked me to proofread her essay. A psychology class, I believe. It was a study about the real and virtual identities of MMO players in which she interviewed a player (not me, which did sting a little – but then again, as you will find out if you keep reading, my answers would probably have wrecked her thesis gloriously) about his experiences with other players, his characters and their creation process, and how the characters he played directly shaped the interactions with the other players. Something along those lines, but I don't really remember what it really tried to demonstrate.

Either way, it got me to thinking about my own real and virtual identities and how they shape my in-game experience. I'm not much of a chatter in MMOs, but I have been known to interact with people. Still, I couldn't reach any concrete conclusion about how my characters affect how I act around other people. Did changing from one character to another cause a shift? Maybe if I played a healer as opposed to a tank, I'd say something more – being at the back of the battle allows more time to type in a few quick words and there's less of a chance I'll royally mess up and stress.

It is probably assumed if you play for a female your interaction will be different than when playing for a male. Maybe that is different for guys more than for me. Then again, I hardly ever play for a male. Females are so much more fun to create. My usual partier, a guy, also plays almost exclusively for females and rarely interacts differently with people. For the most part, probably because he doesn't care enough to change his attitude from one character to another in a chat channel. But he does tell me, "Tell them you're a girl, they'll give you stuff." I've never done it and I doubt that it happens, but it is a running joke they'll flock to you if you tell them you're a girl. You might even be treated with a less explosive attitude if they know you're a "girl", though whether that speaks to sexism or not, I'm not going to get into (neither do I want to treat this subject here, nor do I really care about it if it were true).

I can't speak for everyone else and I won't speak for those interactions conducted while role-playing – assuming the role of your character and shaping your conversation around who your character is as opposed to what you would usually say yourself. But for me and my usual partner, who is really the only other experience I have witnessed, conversations are usually dependent on ourselves with others. Sure, there might be the mean making fun of someone's character or actions harmlessly (and it is obviously so), which is easily facilitated by the anonymity a chat and virtual identity (your character) provide, but there isn't really much of anything else.

As I said, I don't remember enough of my friend's essay to make any generalizing claims with certainty now or even to draw conclusions on my own gameplay style in relation to others. And this won't be the focus of this piece either. What I have noticed, though, when it comes to playing games, which might very well be a restrained experience not common to all players, at least not at the level at which me and my friend take it, is that the greatest part that is influenced when playing is the character itself, players be damned. Identity still plays a huge role but outside the realm of player-player interaction.

I haven't played many RPGs, mainly because I always get distracted from the main quest and want to do my own thing or because the character creation process wasn't satisfying enough. You'll see what I mean about that soon enough. But I have played plenty games where the character is given – you do not create your own and you do not have any opportunity to create its own story. That didn't stop me from getting attached to characters where there is an actual story. I might scream my frustrations and disappointment or excitedly exclaim my satisfaction or even, yes, I admit it, cry when something happens to the character I am playing for or someone else in the story line. I might get unreasonably attached to an NPC and hesitate in killing it, spend time mourning it, or do my best to advance my quest in such a manner that I force a happy result for them, which in turn makes me happy. For some Co-ops, and here I will give the example of Left 4 Dead 2, the character pool is so small (here not counting mods that change a character's appearance to whatever you might like and you might be the only one to know it, unless others use it, too) and there are so many people playing these characters that it becomes difficult to establish a rapport with any character. Most gamers will fight to get the few characters that are really liked (for which there is quite a consensus among the community), while the late comers will bemoan being stuck with the one no one wants. Interactions are conducted completely outside the character itself, who has become a mere avatar with little meaning, which is why my friend's study and those of researchers out there focused on MMOs.

MMOs really allow you to create your own character. Your own persona. I take you back to the first time I created such a character. It was last year, end of March, beginning of April. I'd watched videos, preparing myself, choosing which race and class I would play. I enter the character selection screen. I already know the race and class. I don't know what I

21

will create. Obviously, a female. I cycle through the faces – as usual, the choice is quite limited, but they are good enough. I choose the one that I liked best. Surprisingly, she looks quite punky, which I didn't expect. I'm not one to appreciate the punk style. But she is slowly taking shape. A creature I never envisioned, a creature I never prepared for. I choose her make-up, add one cross earring on her left ear. Painstakingly, I choose a hairstyle, which sadly is bundled with the horns – I cannot choose them independently. But it's good enough. I'm disappointed these devilish people haven't been given a tail – a long, thicker one for the males and a thinner, shorter one for the females.

To me, they have one, it's just not shown.

Seeing her better, a story slowly starts forming in my mind. She is young, she is a warrior, she is still naïve, but not innocent. She has joined the army for glory, having grown up listening to stories about heroes, but knows little about what it means and what it will mean for her. She has no idea what is in store for her and I don't either. The surprise hasn't unfolded entirely. I tweak her features, make her really my own, then I go to the name creation tab. I'm stuck. What do I do? I think and think and think. I always liked the name Rae. I always liked Sailor Moon and in the English dub (which I never watched as it is, sorry, voice actors, awful), Sailor Mars' name is Rae, to be similar to the Japanese Rei. I always liked Sailor Mars – my favorite. But Rae doesn't quite fit this beauty I have here. I keep on thinking. She is ferocious and brave. Reckless, really – being so young and inexperienced, she doesn't know the weight of loss, of sacrifice. The story continues to form as I think on her name. She's a redhead – a vivid, lava-like gorgeous redhead, as it fits her race. Fire. Fire… Rae… And ferocious, right? She strikes fear into the hearts of enemies. Like a wraith. Fire, Rae, Wraith. I have the name. Fyraethe. I am satisfied it is unique and that it fits her.

Over days and weeks of playing her with my friend's character, Binala – a quiet, lonely elf who knows the value of life and the meaning of loss, providing the perfect balance for Fyraethe – both their stories develop. It takes my friend by surprise. "I can't believe we're actually making them stories!" he exclaims one day exasperated with how far we have gone. Today, he loves it. Fyraethe becomes Fyra, her name shortened for convenience, giving proof of their close friendship. Fyra becomes what her parents, removed on a different continent also call her. Her life takes shape behind the scenes, in conversations and musings whenever she comes to mind.

She falls in love with an NPC. I do not, but she does. Her emotions take a life of their own, outside my own control – they just happen and it seems unreasonable for me to try to change them.

I'd been writing stories and fanfictions with another friend for a long time. I knew what it meant to put yourself in a character's shoes and simulate their emotions. I was also used to their emotions running out of my own control. I was no longer the author, I was just a narrator, witnessing their tribulations and feeling everything they did, against my own wishes. Feeling their pain and crying, feeling their joy and smiling like an idiot while no one around me understood why. Crazy, right? I'd say I am. You don't know half the story yet.

I have perhaps a dozen characters split across two MMOs. They all have their own story. They all have a name. They all have their own emotions, their own likes and dislikes. Just the other day, I created my newest character. A beastly one, of a race that is really an animal evolved with intelligence and society, like humans. I perfected him. Fur, fur pattern, hair, horns, facial features, everything. His story slowly takes shape. I need a name. I cannot think of a proper name. All the names that I choose – with the half-exception of one, who shares a clan name with a favorite character from a series – are truly unique. They are their own people in their own right. To me, to my friend, they bleed, they feel, they cry, they get their hearts broken. Now I need to make this one. I sat in front of the screen, thinking for more than an hour. You read that right. More than an hour. Insane, right? I've passed insane long ago and took a left turn down Maniac Boulevard. Finally, I decide on the silliest name such a brute could ever have. He is massive, a giant really, towering over humans by twice their size, with huge fangs and a mean, surreal look in his eyes. (He is also my only male character.) His name is Snowflake Ironforge.

The creation of a character is not what I first expected it to be a year ago. I never assumed I would put so much effort and heart into them. If someone makes a negative comment, even a good-humoured one, I get worked up over it. They have insulted my creation, what I have spent so much time perfecting and developing. They cannot be forgiven and the foul mood (if the comment struck a particularly sensitive nerve) doesn't pass easily. I jump to the defense, whether vocally or not. Everything churns within – I go over everything that the character is, everything that proves the opposite of what was said. I have no children, but it does feel like someone has just insulted my baby.

As I log onto one character, I go into a particular mode. Loading Fyra? I am ready to take every in-game, in-quest action that fits her to the letter. Loading Mei Mae Minn? Initiating crazy, clumsy genius mode. Dahria? Dark, brooding, tough mode – I am the boss, I am vengeful and am not easily impressed.

You get the point, I don't need to go on. Actions are taken, even if I myself would prefer it to be the other way. I feel everything that they feel, even if I wish they felt differently. Even if I wish this character didn't hate her childhood neighbour, because I do like that childhood neighbour. My creations are close to my heart and come to life.

Their life is, to some extent, led outside of me. I have no control over whom they love or hate, what they desire, what they hate or like – while I am the story-teller and answer the question when asked, after serious deliberation, it is always chosen based on who they are. They have clear, distinct identities and, were I to overlook the game's default story, they would all go their different paths. These paths would at some point intersect, for some, not for all.

I would assume some tenet of psychology would say they all share something of me. That their identities are, at the heart of things, stemming from the one thing they have in common – the creator. I cannot find that. Can an author similarly say the characters woven into the story are truly only made possible because a part of them provided the root? Where the root might only really be their imagination and ability to empathize with others to the extent of creating the semblance of life?

I can admit the root found within me, the one thing in common is that I perhaps cannot envision some things that would create different characters. Perhaps some mentalities are impossible for me to recreate. But more than that, I am the root because although they all have their own lives, their own ambitions and desires, these identities are constantly swirling around in my head. My head is a boiling pot, assaulted at the most random of times by these multiple virtual personalities that I have created and lost control of. The one thing that I can say is truly dependent on me is the likelihood of one character to figure in my mind more than another. I can only say it is truly mine this favoritism that makes me feel closer to one character than another, but even then I cannot be sure if it really is my choice. Some grow on me with time, some are cherished so deeply from the very beginning.

I don't know what sense can be made of this virtual identity mania of mine, but I could probably safely say that I have a multiple personality disorder. And it does not include only personalities created for the sake of MMOs. I have been writing stories for the better part of five years – true stories, with fully-fleshed characters, not the short, discarded stories written in high school for class. Over the course of these five years, I have created more characters than I can remember. But those that I do remember are so close and true to my heart. I feel their joy and their disappointment and I bend over backwards to find loopholes or new means of getting them what they want, giving them the chance to become what they have the potential to be.

I have previously said my friend also created such personalities for his characters. But unlike my own, he is in full control of their feelings, their ambitions, and their desires. If he wants it one way, that's the way they'll have it. Something like, "When I want your opinion, I'll give it to you." He cannot comprehend how I am unable to change these personalities and all that makes them what they are. He says, "You are their creator, you should be in control." Maybe I no longer am their creator. Maybe I am now something else.

Creation is important. It is an inherent part of us and what we have created, we will defend tooth and nail. Much like an artist who defends his painting against the howling, humiliating mockery of others, it becomes an intrinsic part of us and it is difficult to let go.

Maybe I am really just a maniac, treasuring these personalities that exist only deep within my mind and heart. Maybe I no longer am a creator, maybe I am just a sufferer of a strange sort of multiple personality disorder. But even if I am, these characters of mine are that amazing that, say what you want, I am damn proud of them.

OPERATION

BY *J.C. CANTIN*

*Author's bio: **J.C.** is a hopeful and currently unpublished Canadian author. Something happened and words appeared. More to follow.*

I operated on a computer last Wednesday. It wasn't the first time; I've now done about ten over the past five years. When I was all done, I felt as though I had accomplished something. I had done something important and of value with my day! In retrospect however, it's not much of an achievement.

For those not familiar with the process, it is a strange one, mixing moments of finesse, brute force, 'oh-shit's and, in my case, blood. I wish I was kidding about that last one.

The process always begins with the case. Mine is a prototypical black box that is far too large to sit under or on my desk. It has all manner of cut outs, perforations and plastic cladding one would expect on most cases. It is well built and well machined. In spite of that it has more sharp edges and rough corners than you would reasonably expect. More importantly, it extracts a price every time I dare to even dream of inspecting its innards through anything but the faded plastic masquerading as a window. The case is also utterly ruthless, without pity or remorse about collecting, and it always expects to be paid up front.

Having pulled out the beast and wrestling it onto its side, I won the initial skirmish at the expense of a cut below my shinbone and one on my finger. Fuck. Hope springs eternal but at least this time they're not deep enough that I'll need bandages.

With payment out of the way, I delved into the heart of the machine establishing my plan of action. My purpose this time was straightforward and seemingly simple, but complex in execution. I was here to replace the central fan, install some RAM and two hard drives. That doesn't sound so bad, right? Let me explain why everything about that last sentence is hugely disingenuous.

First, I will need to remove the original fan from its preferred parking spot atop the computer chip. Barely adequate to the task of drawing away the heat, the new one is a clear upgrade but the work is delicate. The chip is a square roughly the size of a saltine. Costing hundreds of dollars and made of silicon with a metal plate on top, the underside is literally comprised of hundreds of little pins, all of whom have a bespoke socket on the motherboard. Bending one of these pins can, and often does, require the complete replacement of our little silicon wafer. Installing these chips is absolutely nerve-wracking and it makes the most awful grinding sound as it is latched in to the motherboard. Thankfully, I was not here to undertake that task and the original fan was easily dispatched.

Next, I need to remove the motherboard. The motherboard is the spine of the whole machine. Long and flat, with protruding metal and plastic placed with seemingly little rhyme or reason, it's an awkward piece with unequal weight distribution. It's also fastened with 9 of the smallest screws you can imagine.

Dear reader, I am not a small man. I do not have delicate hands.

Cursing my decision to do this at all, I manage to somehow disentangle the motherboard and remove it with minimal mysterious clinking. I only dropped 3 screws, a new record! Corralling all the screws into an easy to find location (some of them reluctant to come as they snag onto the board) I can only hope I haven't broken anything.

I move the board onto a piece of shipping cardboard pretending to be a workbench and consider my next move. The new fan, unlike the old one, has a back plate that needs installing before I can mount the fan. I cannot avoid installing the back plate now but the fan I could install once the board is back in the case. I decide against it as it would be unsecured on its own without the fan installed and I will have my hands full navigating the mess of wiring that remains in the case. In theory, this should be the easy part. Riiight, in theory....

Imagine if you will a multi-level parking garage of 50 stories. Now imagine the engineers had devised a method to split it perfectly

43

in the middle so it becomes two equal towers. They've also managed to remove the outer support pillars so that all the support is provided by a pillar in the middle of the cut, one for each side. Finally, imagine the whole thing a foot tall by 4 inches wide and instead of parking spots, delicate metallic leaves made of the thinnest of metal sheeting sprouting from the central columns. It is properly known as a heatsink and draws the immense heat created by the chip up and into the leaves allowing the fans that hang off of it to cool them in the process. It is exceptionally pretty craftsmanship, beautifully built but very delicate and thus vulnerable to just about any sudden pressure or hit. Oh, and it sits on the brain of the computer, the chip. You know that hyper-sensitive-don't-ruin-it-at-your-own-peril-you've-been-warned-thing I mentioned earlier? Now, I get to attach this delicate monstrosity to the top and pray I don't ruin both in the process!

To make matters worse, there's a thin coating of thermal paste that needs to be removed and replaced before the new heatsink can go on. This, I've never done. Fuck. Normally the custom heatsink is put on when the chip is first installed but for a variety of reasons, it wasn't in the cards then. I wish it wasn't in the cards now.

The solvent came squirting out in higher volume than I anticipated and quickly but unevenly spread across the surface of the chip. Thankfully, by some magic, it didn't spill over the edge down into the socket. I would be a much poorer man today if it had. My first attempted wipe lifts most of the paste. I try again with better results. As I was hesitant to put much pressure or to wipe with any kind of lateral force though, smudges remained. This was a problem as I still had to put on a second solvent and the new paste. I stop here for a moment to contemplate my options and was reminded of a quip one of my good and long-lost friends was so fond of.

'In for a Penny, in for a Pound'

So, resolving to deal with the consequences, I try a third time with a bit more vigor. The grinding of my teeth was matched only by that the chip. They still hurt. There's no way to check for damage at this stage, so on I went.

The heatsink fit beautifully onto the back plate's protruding pins and I lower it onto the chip, the new thermal paste not squelching as anticipated. It really is an astounding piece of engineering. Threading the special screw-driver down between the towers, I begin to tighten the screws onto their fittings. Any give at all will cause problems. It slips. The screwdriver falls. Not once, but twice as I try to secure the screws as tight as they will go. Remember, I do not have delicate hands. Thankfully, I don't damage the leaves. Hopefully, I didn't damage anything else.

Feeling the motherboard flex under the added weight, I swiftly but carefully load it back into the case. Back on its mounts, I begin the process of screwing it back into the case. I only dropped 2 screws this time but had a small moment of panic when I realized I had to tip the case to recover one of them.

For those keeping track, that's five 'oh-shit's' so far.

Navigating the case to connect all the cabling around the monstrosity now permanently perched above my chip was an interesting experience but thankfully without incident. The installation of the two sizeable fans that accompanied the heatsink is also without trouble. I'm learning all about due care and attention as I go. The drives were similarly installed without much in the way of excitement. Sure I miscalculated and had to rewire the whole section but that's barely worth mentioning. Why do I keep doing this to myself?

The ram on the other hand, was not without incident. In general, it's a simple install. One I've done dozens of times over the past twenty years. It's potentially the easiest thing to do. The general process is to line up the stick with the appropriate slot and push and push and push until the plastic fittings click into place. To be clear, it's no small effort. The whole board flexes underneath. It's a bit surreal at first but you quickly become accustomed to it. Well, as it turned out this time, I hadn't lined it up; I was pushing it directly into the space between the fittings.

Here I was pushing and pushing, waiting for the click to confirm it was seated and nothing was coming. Furthermore, in my haste I had put pressure on the module next to the one I was trying to put in causing it to lean far more than I was comfortable. Oh-shit. After all that work earlier, was I going to ruin it all on the home stretch? Pulling out the stick, I inspect it, the one next to it and the board. No sign of stress, thankfully. I line up again and it goes in without incident, confirming it is now seated with a satisfying click.

There's no need to waste time reviewing my work. It's either done and it works or it's not and it fails. Computers won't wait around to tell you. You'll know right away. I plug in the bare necessities and make my way to the power button. I pause a moment. There's always a small hesitation.

What if it catches fire or worse yet, is unresponsive?

Penny and Pound and all that, I take a breath and push the button.

51

Life!

I have it cycle a few times, self-diagnose and stress test it. It's working. That it does so without errors or failures is the cherry on top.

Quickly, panels on, wrestle it back into place before it changes its mind!

You might be thinking, 'so what? That's it?' As I wrote earlier, it's not much of an accomplishment. The computer has no productivity software of any kind and is used mainly as a glorified internet, Netflix, videogames machine and an expensive one at that. I didn't even write this piece on it! For my two hours of work, it'll run flawlessly (I hope) for about five years and I'll go through the whole thing again. Writing this took much longer and will prove to be equally unimportant in the long run. I'm perfectly content with that knowledge however as the purpose of the exercise, the story and this piece, was to highlight the accomplishment we can find in those little things we love doing even if they serve no greater purpose. There's value in that on a deeply personal level.

THIRD AWARD

BUDGET CUTS

BY *LILIAN LEE*

Author's Bio: **Lillian Lee** – *wannabee writer, single mother and handicapped budget maker*

There are some hard times out there. Hard times call for adjustments and budgeting especially when you're a single mom with a very limited income. When you're also young or at least believe yourself in that category still, you have to be creative to keep up with fashion and with the people around.

The problem comes when you've never really learnt how to budget what you have and how to do everything you could to make ends meet.

I thought hard and came up with a solution: I will start making my own clothes. In a way or another, I will manage to save money and to keep up with the changes in the world around me.

First try: a beautiful yellow dress with huge leaves splattered all over the place. I saw the fabric in a store nearby and I had an interesting model in my mind: it was simple and sassy. No big deal, I thought and I made the calculations and saw that I would actually save quite a lot of money by buying the fabric and sew the dress myself.

I measured myself and then I measured the fabric, not once but at least three times to be sure. I cut through the fabric with the model in mind and then I started sewing the pieces together. It was hard work, requiring a lot of patience and that is something that I don't have in high supply in stock. However, I persevered.

After days of painstakingly sewing with care so no one could see the dress was handmade, I finished it and I was in terrible awe. It looked as great as I thought it would. Then, the disappointment hit: it didn't fit me.

I tried to put it on but it was a lost battle. It seemed that the measurements were somehow skewed.

For a moment there, I thought to cut it and make a skirt out of it. I could have used parts of the fabric from the top to insert panels in the skirt.

I couldn't do it. The dress was too fluid and too elegant to be messed with. With a sigh of regret, I offered it to my sister who is about thirty pounds lighter than I. The dress looked perfect on her, and not only the color or the pattern but also the model.

So, that was strike one. My budget was more burdened and I was in the red.

Then I thought I'd try something else. Knitting seemed harmless and I had control over the size. The only setback was the fact that I had never learnt how to knit. When it came to that, it looked like I had two left hands.

That didn't stop me. I borrowed a book from the library. It spelled everything out and also offered ideas. I chose something not very difficult but not very simple either. I was looking for class as well, not only for economy.

It took me a few days to learn how to start. If I were to be honest, I should say that it took me about two weeks. Then I started knitting following the model in the book.

I was thinking of knitting a blouse that would work in spring and in autumn as well, but that could be worn also in summer if I had a chance to go to the mountains. Fat chance that but I always thought it was better to dream and hope than to let yourself drown in melancholy.

I worked hard for a few more weeks. The progress was steady even though quite minimal. Finally I got to the sleeves part. That sank me.

I tried everything in my power, I counted and I checked the book again. By now, I had already had to borrow it twice. Nothing worked. I knitted and then, I started all over again a few times. In the end, I decided to ask for help so I went to an aunt and asked her how to do the sleeves.

She lectured for about an hour and half. My eyes grew glassy and my mind went numb. I couldn't follow the lecture that was embellished with all sorts of advice on housework matters. I hoped at least that she'd start working on the sleeves and then, with my analytical mind – who am I kidding? I don't really have an analytical mind - I could replicate what she did. However, she didn't. She only lectured.

I left her house with a terrible headache and with an unsolved problem.

Nevertheless, I decided not to throw the towel yet. I went home and took out my little black book and started going through all the people I knew. I was sure I could find at least one who would be able to help me.

After another hour, I had to give up. There was no one there. None of my friends would have had the time or inclination to knit.

The next step was to take the phone and call one of my close friends to complain about the impossibility of finding a way to be well dressed and preserve my miser budget as well. I told her about my try to knit the blouse and my inability to pass over the sleeves. And then she stunned me. She told me her husband was a genius when it came to knitting and that he would be happy to help me.

I don't really know how happy he was, but I ran immediately to their house, not to lose my chance of finishing at least that blouse.

Indeed, he was a genius at knitting. However, he was far away from a genius when it came to explaining. In the end, exhausted and exasperated, he gave up showing me and he knitted the sleeves himself. He had speed and accuracy. I couldn't even see the moves. Everything was blurry.

I was very grateful. The only thing to do now was to sew the entire thing up and I would have had a blouse. He asked me though not to come back with any knitting projects and that brought an end to my knitting adventure.

So, I went back to analyzing the budget to see what I could do to save and still feel like I had everything I wanted.

After a few more days of creating columns and trying to reason with the figures that didn't want to cooperate with me at all, I realized that there was only one way if I wanted to be in the budget: to say good bye to some of the things. No more new clothes at the beginning of the season, not that I had ever bought more than one or two, but anyway; no more going out every Saturday evening, because I had to choose between that and my son's hockey practice, and no more second coffees during my work program. I had to live with one.

I had to hand the victory to the gloomy budget and to skulk away defeated. Nevertheless, I will come up with something that would help me enjoy life in a way or another.

SHORT-STORY AWARD

FIRST PRIZE

THE SHADOW

By *Lucian Arthur*

*Author's Bio: **Arthur** is what many call a fanatic of murder mysteries. Living in Ontario's Near-North for most of his 58 years, he spends much of his free time since retirement watching, taking in and writing about the shadowy goings on of fictitious everyday Canadians. This is his first foray into publication.*

That morning, he woke up with a sharp gasp and an idea stuck in his mind. He rubbed his eyes with hairy, thick knuckles – a woman once had told him that they seemed to belong to an ape. Then, he just relaxed.

Yeah, why the hell not? It was a good idea, actually, a great idea, after all. He'd strike two flies with the same blow.

The move was smart and long overdue. He'd been thinking a lot about doing something but he was smart enough not to put his neck into the noose. His burning wish was for revenge not suicide.

Energized, he jumped out of bed and went into the small bathroom. Everything around him was skimpy. He had downsized everything since that fatidic morning. Had he downsized more, he'd have vanished completely.

Huh, living off the grid had his perks. No one could trace his moves, and, more than that, no one really knew if he existed. Or to be accurate, no one knew if he still existed anymore.

He started shaving, driving the blade closely to the skin, careful not to leave marks on his face. People remembered a goatee, a shaved skull with a tattoo at the back, and now he managed to move around without shaking any memories loose. No one had seen him like that since he enlisted ten years ago.

He looked at himself in the mirror, and for the first time in the last four months, he could look at himself, into his eyes, without shame or guilt. He finally had a plan.

She had died in that dirty alley, behind the smelly dumpster, rain slapping her face furiously, wind playing with the hair splattered with blood, her lifeless eyes staring at the overcast sky. And while she was dying, crying and probably begging for mercy or help, he was drinking his mind in a bar not far away.

He'd thought he'd have time to reconnect with her and to do all the things he'd put on hold for ten years. He'd thought he deserved a night with friends he'd not seen for too long to dwell on the years that had already passed and to get shitfaced like a stupid teenager in a feat of rebellion.

Choices! In the end, all that was, it was choices. Or mistakes. Or fate. Or the hell knows what. The bottom line was that she had died there because he'd been too bent on drinking beer and boasting like a stupid teenager with the eye only on the moment not on the bigger picture. He had to pay a price in the end but not before the actual killers would pay theirs.

***

He already knew the woman's schedule. She'd sleep all morning, getting up somewhere after noon, with a raging hangover and pissed off that life would deal her some shitty cards. Then, she would yell a bit at the kids playing in the yard across the street, their yelling cutting like a blade through her numb brain. Then she would start prowling the streets, looking for the next dude able to buy her enough drinks to keep her living through the night. In the wee hours of the morning, she'd return home – if that shackled house could be called home, and she'd turn into bed, without even taking off her scruffy boots and the clothes smelling of cheap booze and smoke.

He'd visited her house in the past and she hadn't winked. He'd been careful not to leave any trace of his passing and to survey all the exits and the vantage points from the street and houses nearby. Her back door was opening over a yard full of junk and beyond the back fence, there were the rail tracks. No one to see him coming and going. This time, his purpose was very precise: he'd seen her using the big kitchen knife a few times and once she'd even nicked her finger cutting into stale bread. She hadn't bothered to wash it afterwards and he doubted she'd done it later on. The blood should have been on that blade if not on the hilt: exactly what he needed to see the job done.

He put on a pair of thick surgical gloves and lifted the knife. He checked the traces of blood and the corners of his mouth smirked: the blood was still there as he'd expected. Just fine for what he had in mind. He bagged the knife in a clean plastic bag he'd just torn from a roll he'd brought with him and then took her soiled jacket and put it into another bag.

He looked around surveying the space, saw that nothing was out of place and that he'd left nothing behind. Only then, he left.

Now he had to move faster. He was working against the clock and he couldn't do a rush job if he wanted them to pay. Rushing too much would mean losing attention on the details and having one of them escaping their fate and that wouldn't do. They had to pay for what they'd done.

Initially he'd tried the police but that lazy detective couldn't move his ass fast enough and couldn't be bothered to check something that was not screaming in his face. He'd already taken care of him. He'd messed with his head for a few months, scared him to death and helped him hallucinate a great deal – after all, he knew exactly what drug to use and how often so that the big fat lazy detective couldn't run away from what it was pre-ordained in his destiny. He'd finally made use of his service gun and put a 9 mm through his skull. It'd been a neat job even though there'd been blood everywhere. He'd seen everything from his hiding place using a very strong lens.

Now, everything had to come to an end. He'd finally mastered the plan to get the best results and have the best revenge. The one that had used the knife on his girlfriend would die by the knife. The one that instigated the murder and the desecration of that sweet woman's life would go behind bars for the rest of her fucking life.

***

He knew where to find him as he'd cased the joint for a few months already. It'd been difficult to pinpoint the exact moment when he'd find him alone as he was living in a house with two other guys but his work was made easier because the other two started working in a scrap garage and in the mornings they were busy there.

He knew he'd find him with his brains full of the vapor of the alcohol. He'd have preferred to find him sober so that he could be sure that he'd grasp the significance of his early demise but he couldn't bank on that. He was rarely sober and even then just

77

for a short time and usually when he was surrounded by people. His plan didn't allow for other people's presence.

It was a dump in a very "nice" neighborhood. Luckily, mornings were not very animated and he'd learned to be one with the environment. However, this time, he didn't want any kind of doubt concerning the killer.

He entered through the back door, which was always open. It would have been difficult to lock it as the door couldn't be closed. The jamb had been nicked in the past and there was no way to close the door. In winter, it must have been a living hell with the chilly air coming in. The southern location of the town made it easy, he supposed. No blizzards like the ones in the east or snow.

After getting inside, he listened for any noise that would warn him that other people were there but heard nothing. He stopped in the kitchen to put on his thick gloves and to wrap the soiled jacket he'd taken from the woman's house around his body over the plastic he'd already covered himself with. It was a little small but blood splatter would be found on it anyway, so no big deal.

He advanced silently on the corridor leading to the room he knew by heart now and opened the door.

The intended victim was lying on his stomach with his arms folded underneath, exactly in the position he'd fallen in the bed.

He jerked his head up, slapped him soundly and pressed the knife over the skin of his cheek, from the eye to the corner of his mouth. Blood surged and trickled on the pillow. A growl of pain emerged and his eyelids shot up.

"What the fuck…"

He couldn't finish as a low voice said:

"You'd better shut up, asshole! This is judgement day and you have to

reckon all your sins before going to
meet your maker!"

He found delight in seeing the
fear swimming in the pools of the eyes
full of tears.

"Do you remember little
Juanita?"

For a moment, it seemed that
Juanita's memory had been erased
from the killer's mind but then,
something clicked, and understanding
brought animalistic fear in his eyes.
He tried to get away but the blade of
the knife left a mark on his throat, not
deep enough to kill but deep enough to
hurt.

"Juanita was a sweet girl who'd done nothing to you! Because that bitch's boyfriend tried to charm her, she had you kill her but first you had to torture her to satisfy the bitch. Well, now, it is your turn," he said slashing a line through the shirt over the killer's (soon-to-be a victim) chest.

The man trashed around trying to escape but the force of the arm holding him down was too much for him. He started yelling, with each slash, till a final move slashed his throat. Blood gushed out, staining the woman's jacket.

He got off the bed and checked for blood anywhere around the bed. It wouldn't do leave any bloody prints around, even though he'd taken the caution to cover his shoes with plastic shoes, like the ones used in the hospital. It was a good thing to know a woman or two working in a hospital. Satisfied that there was no danger to do that, he went to the kitchen and carefully bagged the bloody jacket. Then he took off the plastic and bagged it. He checked every piece of his clothing, took off the plastic covering his shoes, the shower cap he'd covered his hair with and checked everything around to be sure he'd left nothing of himself behind.

He left the house through the same back door and in a few minutes reached the old rusty truck he'd left on a side street. He drove to the woman's house and carefully got inside and left the jacket on the sofa. He left silently and drove to the other end of the town where he threw the bloody plastics in a dumpster.

Then, he came back towards downtown. Downtown, he stopped his car and placed the call.

"911, what's your emergency?"

"I want to report a crime, I think," he said with a high-pitched voice. "I saw a woman coming out of a house on …. Street, from number 10 and she had blood on her. She was behaving strangely. I've seen her before although lately she hasn't come around so much. Her name is Cissy

Dollan, I think. I know she lives on …. Street."

"What's your name?"

"No, no, no. No name. Just my duty", he stammered and put the receiver down.

The area was crowded enough and no one was paying attention to him. He started walking down the street towards his car. His step was lazy like he had no hurry or worry in the world. Well, he didn't. He'd already taken care of that.

***

The next evening, having a beer in front of the TV, he heard the News speaker saying:

"The police made an arrest in the killing of Harry Camden. They arrested Cissy Dolan and she will be charged with first degree murder. Police sources intimated that there was a similarity with the death of Juanita Gonzales and they want to move towards charging Dolan with her death as well".

Finally, he released a raspy breath and murmured: "At last, I got your revenge, babe!"

SECOND PRIZE

THE LOVE OF MY LIFE - NEVER TOO LATE

By *Aleena Dumovski*

*Author's Bio: Born to Russian parents, **Aleena** was just three when her family immigrated to England 55 years ago. Aleena currently lives in Islington with her 3 lovebirds and enjoys writing well embellished semi-accurate biographical accounts of her most interesting life. You'll be pleased to hear that since the 'incident' Aleena has managed to avoid getting her skirt caught in her underthings.*

I met the love of my life in late spring. Too bad: it was one-sided. I don't think it could have been different considering how I met him.

I left my apartment to go to university and there he was, in the elevator. I'd heard a real hunk had moved in the apartment two doors down from mine. I smiled to him showing my straight rows of whites and I could see a playful light in his eyes. Instantly, I thought: that was it.

He was exactly what I'd imagined I'd want during all those awkward years of looking around, trying to find my Mr. Right and being shut down just because I had those ugly braces, the height and the curves of a scarecrow and the chest of a boy. Well, that changed. The braces were gone leaving behind a beautiful smile, the height remained but got assorted with curves and my breast sprouted and I was filling a double D bra. Now, I had my chance to have my Mr. Right.

I smiled wider and tried to get a bit closer, maybe, maybe he'd do a move. I know everything about flirting from movies and erotic novels. Besides reading for my courses, that's what I do: I read erotic novels, watch chick flicks and steal advice from Cosmo. Even now, even though it doesn't seem like it matters anyway. I suppose it became a habit.

He simply laughed and for a moment there I felt unsure. The elevator reached ground floor. He let me pass first and followed me out. I had already been out of the door of the building when he touched my arms and said:

"I think I'd better let you know: your skirt got caught in your panties."

My cheeks got red. I could feel the rush of blood filling every poor of my skin. I was mortified and then I tried to save face. I laughed as if it had been a common occurrence and playfully touched his arm.

"It happens, doesn't it? Thanks for telling me!" I pulled the skirt out of my panties and tried to console myself that at least I'd showcased my shapely legs and round behind. Nothing to be ashamed of!

He laughed and left.

That was the turning moment, I think. I started checking the hall through the peephole before going out. I was mortified to meet him again. I did everything in my power to avoid him and threw myself into a life full of activity, lying to myself that I had a huge group of friends, a fulfilled life and that there weren't enough hours in a day to do everything I could do.

Now, drinking a Napoleon and watching the people passing by the little bistro in St-Germain, I realize the emptiness I surrounded myself with. The love of my life is stuck somewhere in the past and I didn't even let anyone getting too close. The closest a man got to me was to take my coat off.

Well, I've got so much knowledge and it's going to waste because I've been afraid of being caught with my pants down. Literally!

Swallowing the last of my cognac, I make a decision. The first one coming down this way is mine. Even if he's young or too young! When you turned 55, it doesn't really matter how young he is. I'll turn into a cougar. So what?

A thirty something comes along: black-ink hair, a little longer than the norm, a supple gait and a predatory smile. All right, he's got something in common with the love of my life. So he's he the one I need now.

I cross my legs pushing my skirt farther up my long legs and lean against the back of the chair to push my breasts up. I make a stand. I see his eyes darting towards the buttons almost ready to pop and then lingering over the curve of my hip towards the length of my legs. He licks his lips. Yeah, he's caught. Now, let's try to recapture the lost youth.

THIRD PRIZE

THE BUILDING

By *Mira Popescu*

*Author's Bio: Romanian born and bred, somewhere in the center of Transylvania, **Mira** coquetted with the idea of writing for a long time; however her fear of rejection made every attempt to publish fold. Finally, she imagined that if she could face randy teenagers everyday as an English teacher, she could face not making it on a top spot. Obsessed with what made people tick, she's portraying characters that catch her eye.*

The little block of flats had been erected somewhere after the Second World War and displayed a sedated architecture. It had avoided the modern, post-modern, and neo-classical style and found itself harboring the traditional style that was outdated at the time.

It was hidden behind some old oaks and some bushes whose name I can't remember for the life of me. It boasted only six little apartments but they were all filled with so much life that it was like it was busting at the seams.

The financial worth of the lot beneath the building tripled its value in the last five years and it became evident that the owner was thinking about selling it. Its value was higher than the entire building.

Besides all of that, the building had become a money eater. Plumbing giving in and walls screaming for repairs and new paint were only just a few of the money pits dancing in front of the owner's eyes, who would grind his teeth thinking of what was expected of him.

He'd just inherited the building: there were no connections and no memories. People inside were just names on the renting contracts and those contracts were due for renewal in a month but he hadn't given them a thought. He was dreaming about a fat bank account that would fuel a trip to the tropics, where he'd buy a beautiful cabana somewhere near the beach and drink, swim, and sleep his days away, chasing a female now and then. Heaven on earth, in his peanut-sized brain dosed with the mirage of wealth.

Meanwhile, life was flowing in the little building, hidden by the curtain of trees, sheltered, not a part of the changes that came and went on the principal artery, just a few feet away.

On the second floor, there were three families. They'd been there for almost half a century and had let the changes pass them by.

The apartment on the right hand was inhabited by a seventy-some-old couple. They had moved there immediately after their wedding day, exactly a decade and one day after the end of the big conflagration. They'd been young at the time and many had even said they'd been too young to marry and that the marriage wouldn't last. I guess they'd proved them wrong. Their marriage had already celebrated the fifty-eighth year of marriage and they'd brought up together a passel of children that gave them another passel of grandchildren.

Their days were quiet. They'd wake up early in the morning and had their tea with a slice of bread and jam on the balcony, listening to the birds and breathing the crisp air that came with the dawn. They wouldn't say a word. In so many years, everything had been said and what they needed they could convey with their eyes or a gesture or a sigh. They'd linger on the balcony for a while. He would read the paper and she would just watch the trees in front of the balcony, deep in thought. She'd probably think of her children or of her grandchildren or of something that had happened long, long time ago, far too long for her to remember accurately. After a couple of hours, they'd go out heading towards the market, even if they needed anything or not. It was like a physical exercise for them, to keep them going. They'd have lunch always on the balcony, just a soup or sometimes a soup and a sandwich. She'd cook the soup just before lunch so that they'd eat something fresh. After lunch, they'd sleep for a couple of hours and then they'd go for a walk but in the opposite direction from the market. There was a park nearby, somewhere in the area of 800 feet. They'd rest on a bench for a while and then they'd tour the park. They'd go back after a couple of hours because they never knew when one of the kids would visit and those were the most precious moments of their life. They'd wait at home, in silence, each one reading something and waiting. When night would fall, they'd go to bed to start everything all over again the following day, without thinking that they might not have too many nights left to be spent there.

They'd sleep without hearing a peep even though the apartment next to them was quite a noisy one. The building was solid, though, and isolation good.

The middle apartment on the second floor was rented by a couple in their mid-forties. They'd married about fifteen years before, for the first time. They'd divorced after the first two years and had had a very quarrelsome interlude for about a year when they'd decided to get married again. They'd fought like crazy for about five days a week, screaming at each other and throwing things. Luckily, none of them had been very good in reaching the target so there were no wounds to deal with, but of course they'd had to buy new dishes twice a month till they agreed to buy camping dishes, those made of metal that would withstand the vicious meeting with a wall. The other two days of the week had been the make-up days, when they'd have sex with the same vivacity they used for fighting. The neighbors would have been grateful that the walls were so thick, had they heard what was going on.

The second marriage had lasted a little longer. They'd tried hard and managed to stay married for five years. Then, one day, just because he'd left the toilet lid up, she'd decided it was too much and thrown him out of the house, literally, opening the door and pushing him out. His clothes followed through the window. She asked for a divorce the following day.

The ink hadn't even dried well on the divorce papers, that they found out that they were so in love that they couldn't live one without the other. They'd left the court and flew to Vegas, and in three days they got married again.

Their life was full: rants about everything under the sun, with swearing, yelling, throwing things and resentments building up from Monday to Friday. Friday night, suddenly, everything turned into romance at first, starting with a candle dinner – funny romantic dinner with camping dishes, by the way, and ending with carnal pursuits pigmented with loud moans and screams that would have turned the neighbors' ears red.

Of course, there was no thought about losing their apartment. There wouldn't have been time, even if they'd known.

Unaware of the drama going on in the middle apartment, the family in the other corner apartment on the second floor was living life working hard and raising three children in two rooms. Both were hard-working people and he even held two jobs. They'd been living in that apartment since a month after their wedding when a distant uncle had found out that the apartment had become available. He hadn't mentioned that someone had been brutally killed there, but it might not have mattered. With the rent prices out there, this had seemed like a gift from the heavens.

Their days were spent with running to work, working as many hours as possible to be able to feed the brood of children and to pay rent, electricity, and maybe, if the Lord was benevolent, to save some money for a vacation sometime in the distant future. Then they'd share chores and supervise homework and fall into bed like logs. They wouldn't even have time to think about marital relations. Anyway, the neighbors would take care of their part too.

Being forced to leave the little apartment would have been a hardship. The rents out there were too high and they wouldn't be able to rent anything decent. However, they continued with their hard life unaware of anything happening behind the scenes.

On the first floor, there were three other families. Maybe saying families is too much.

On the left-hand corner, the apartment hid the most mysterious tenant. Tall, broad-shouldered, tanned and dressed in well-pressed clothes, a man in his thirties would live in his own world. He wouldn't know anything about the old couple living above his apartment or the rambunctious couple on the second floor. Hell, he didn't even know the neighbor next to him, and their patios were separated only by a fragile, white picket fence.

He kept strange hours and would be away for days and nights in a row or would spend a few days inside going out only on the patio, to enjoy the sunlight and the breeze.

He'd found the perfect building to rent an apartment. Strangely, there were no old people minding other people's business or women already past their prime trying to offer him either a night in their bedroom or to cook a delicious cake, stealing their way into his heart through his stomach. No one paid attention. He could practice his profession without fearing that someone might see something or hear something or might leak some info to people that shouldn't know anything.

He was a very well-paid gigolo, making his living on the dance floors of the clubs, turning an older woman in his arms, knowing that later she'd find the perfect gift for him, or in a hotel bedroom, offering spinsters the night of their life in exchange for a monetary gift that would pay his rent and a few whims along the way. His eyes were on the money prize and lost everything else from sight. He couldn't guess that his little slice of happiness on earth was about to go. He'd be at a loss for a reaction. He was used to things that went his way without a hitch.

The apartment in the middle of the first floor was the quietest of all, not that any of them would have been noisy. The sturdy construction didn't allow sounds to travel too far. However, this one was quieter than a tomb that wasn't hunted by the owner.

The renter was unknown to the others. He'd come now and then, always under the cover of night. Not even the landlord could have reached him. His application showed the name of John Smith but it was not the name he was born with or the name he'd ever use. He had too many names to count. He didn't have a job of leisure. He was good at tracking people, learning their habits and killing them for a hefty amount of money. He'd be pissed off to learn about the landlord's plans and he'd fulfill a contract without pay for the first time in his life.

The last apartment on the right corner of the first floor was occupied by two old women, mother and daughter. They wouldn't speak to each other anymore and not because they'd learnt each other's thoughts but because they hated each other with a passion. The mother wouldn't drink or eat anything her daughter touched, fearing poisoning. After how much she managed to control and ruin her daughter's life and her chance at a little happiness, she knew she had to be very careful.

They shared a kitchen and a bathroom. The living room would stay empty days and even weeks in a row. Each of them would spend their lives separately in their bedroom.

The mother would crunch chocolates and read thrillers, enjoying the novels where the culprit would go away without a scratch.

The daughter would spend her days dreaming of other times, sometimes reading a romance and crying watching soap operas. Spineless, she'd let her mother chase away every chance she had for a different life and when she'd woken up there was no chance left. She was stooping, her hair was thin and kept falling and her skin was paste white, spotted by the traces of the tears that had become a common occurrence in her daily life.

The mother would have been angry finding out she'd have to move out but she knew nothing. The daughter didn't care. She was past any care in the world.

They all would go on like guinea pigs in a cage, following the paths of their lives, their eyes on tomorrow, without knowing that tomorrow would bring such a big shock that their lives would change forever. Tomorrow lay in the hands of a new owner with the eyes on the horizon, dreaming of a boat, a hut and drink covered by a colorful umbrella without knowing he was harboring a very skilled killer who wouldn't like to have his little nest taken away.